For Mondelene,

For all you do to help students learn to love to read.

Books can be best friends, always there for you.

Your new found friend,
Doris McClellan

BAXTER BADGER'S HOME

WRITTEN BY DORIS MᶜCLELLAN

ILLUSTRATED BY VICKI DIGGS

Hendrick-Long Publishing Co.

P.O. Box 25123 • Dallas, TX 75225

Hello, I am Baxter Badger!

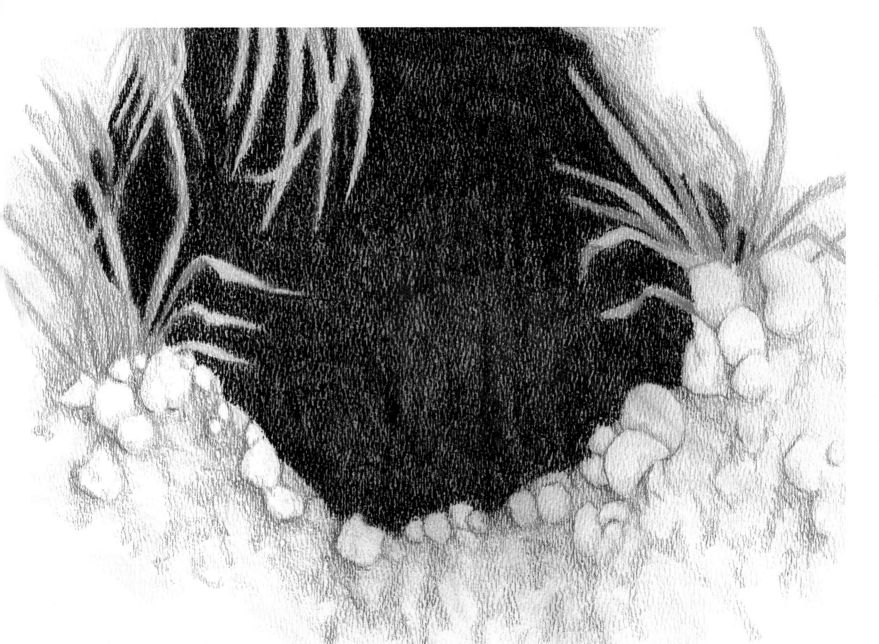

This is my home, which is sometimes called a *BURROW*, or a *SET*.

It takes a lot of digging to make my home. The ground is hard.
First, I use my powerful front legs and sharp claws to dig down.

When the hole starts to get full of loose dirt, I have to back myself out. I push the dirt out behind me with my seat, like a *BULLDOZER*.

Since I can't see where I'm going, the dirt may pile up on the left side of the hole.

Or the dirt may pile up on the right side of the hole.

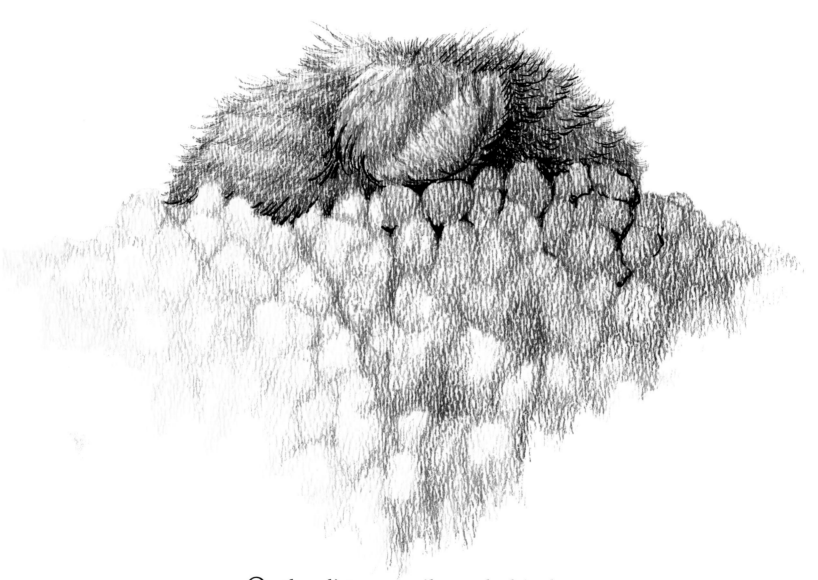

Or the dirt may pile up behind me.

Sometimes, I dig a back door for myself. Also, I dig a shallow
hole nearby to use for my bathroom. I like a clean house.

When it is cold, I stay in my good warm home. In fact, I sleep in my hole all day, so this is why you don't see me very often. But if this sounds like a badger is through digging when his hole is finished, this is not true. Don't believe it!

I also dig for food. My favorite things to eat are *PRAIRIE DOGS*, *EARTHWORMS*, *GROUND SQUIRRELS*, *MICE* and *GOPHERS*. Once . . .

after hunting and hunting for food all night long,

I started walking back home in the morning. Thinking of home and sleep was all that kept me *WADDLING* along.

Near my home, I smelled something strange. This was something I'd smelled before. But what?

Carefully, I edged toward my hole. I came a little closer and started to go into my home. There was a warning Sssssssssss . . .

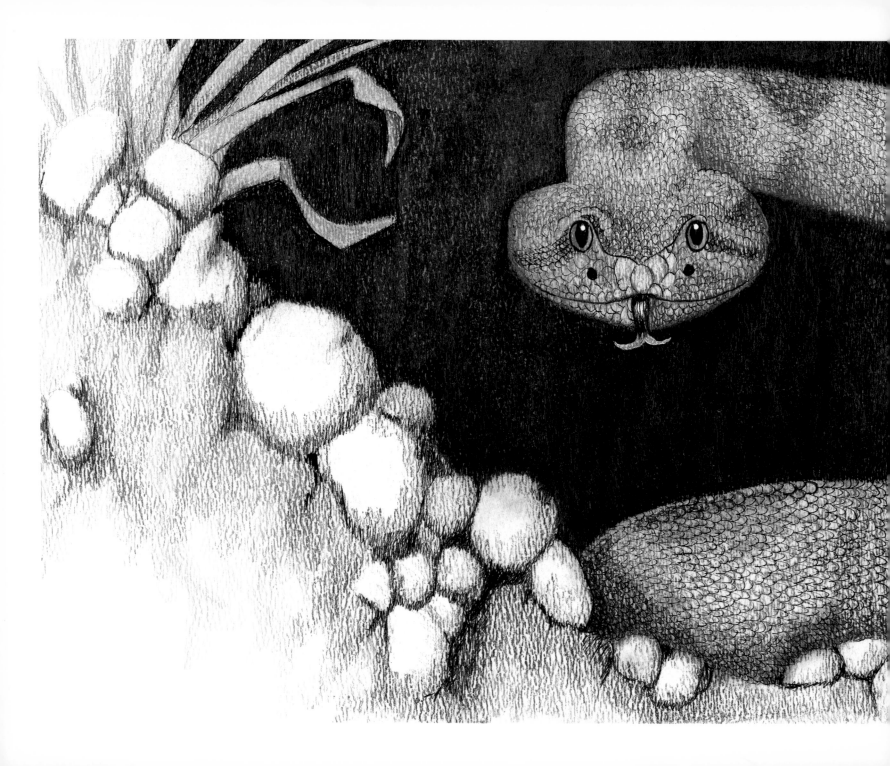

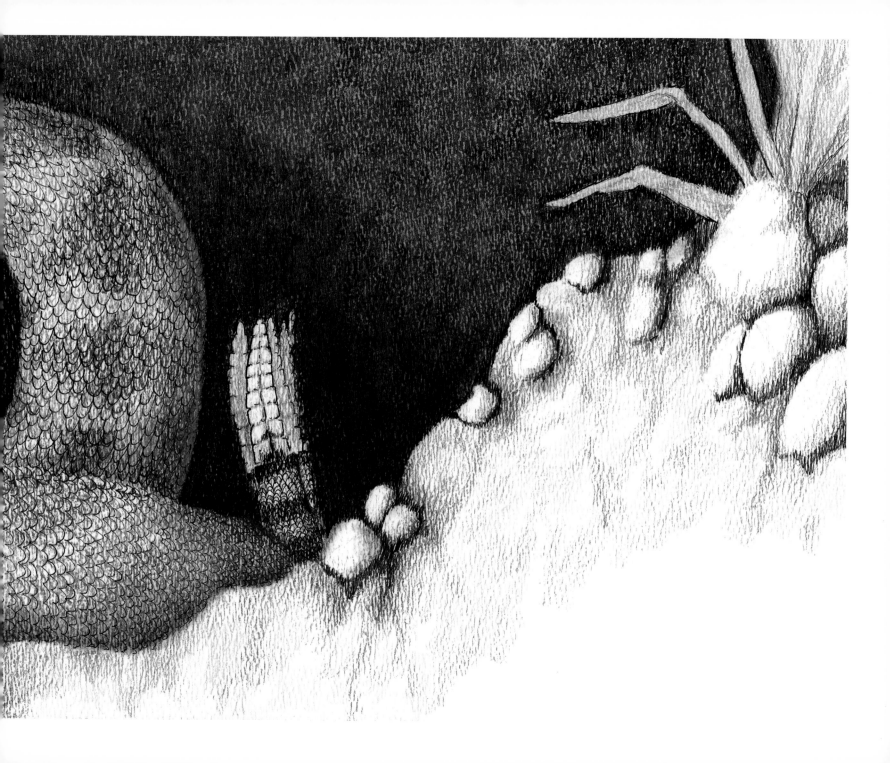

A rattlesnake! Grrrrrrrrr —
I growled at him and puffed
myself up to look twice as
big as I really am!

Still, the rattler did not move. I *LUNGED* at him . . . but not too close. I didn't want to get in striking distance!

ENRAGED, I made a sudden, loud hissing-growling sound and lunged at the same time! I *GNASHED* my teeth and gave off a strong odor. Still, he would not move.

Now, I'm just as brave and strong as the next fellow, but how else is a badger to get a rattlesnake away from his home? I decided to go dig another hole.

Another morning, I came home to find that a coyote had moved in.
She had dug a bigger opening and made what is called a *CLEAN-OUT*.

Now, I thought that coyote was lazy. People call them *WILY*.
Badger *BOARS* and *SOWS* dig their own holes for their *CUBS*.
But that coyote had had her *PUPS* right there in my home!

Again, I had to dig another hole for my home. A badger couldn't just move those babies out of their *DEN*. Besides, coyotes have fleas. My clean home was ruined! If only that coyote had given me a fair fight and left the babies out of it.

When a rattlesnake,

a dog,

or a person tries to hurt me, . . . I try first to scare my enemies away, . . . but I can claw and bite!

I can be a *FEROCIOUS* fighter. But . . .

I'd rather be home feeling safe and cozy!

THE END

Glossary

BOAR: male badger, father

BULLDOZER: a machine with a large blade or ram for pushing

BURROW: badger's home or a hole in which he lives

CLEAN-OUT: coyote's home

COZY: snug, comfortable

CUBS: young badgers; two or three babies born in the spring

DEN: coyote's home or a hole in which he dens

EARTHWORMS: long, slender worms that live in damp dirt

ENRAGED: angry, mad

FEROCIOUS: savage, fierce

GNASH: to grind teeth together

GOPHERS: rodents that live underground

GROUND SQUIRRELS: rodents with short fur and cheek pouches that live underground

LUNGE: to leap forward suddenly

MICE: small rodents with pointed noses, small ears, long bodies and slender tails

PRAIRIE DOGS: rodents that live underground

PUPS: young coyotes

SET: badger's home or a hole in which he lives

SOW: female badger, mother

WADDLING: walking with short steps swaying from side to side

WILY: deceiving, cunning, sly, crafty

Bibliography

Bertin, Leon. *The New Larousse Encyclopedia of Animal Life*. New York: Larousse and Co., Inc., 1980.

Crump, Donald J., ed. *National Geographic Book of Mammals*. Washington, D.C.: National Geographic Society, 1981.

Encyclopedia of the Animal World. Hong Kong: Mandarin Publishers Ltd., 1972.

Familiar Mammals—North America. The Audubon Society Pocket Guides. New York: Alfred A. Knopf, Inc., 1988.

The World Book Encyclopedia. USA: World Book, Inc., 1986.

About the Author

Doris McClellan and her husband, Bill, work for and live on the Spade Ranch, south of Colorado City, Texas. Spade Ranches have been under the same ownership for over 100 years. As a ranch wife, Ms. McClellan enjoys riding side-saddle, riding astride, working cattle and sheep, reading, cooking, and photographing wildflowers and animals. *Baxter Badger's Home* is based on her hours of observation, on horseback and afoot, of the badger and his fellow West Texas "critters." Ms. McClellan is a member of American National Cattlewomen, Inc. and the Ranching Heritage Association. She taught fifth grade for 15 years before earning a master's degree in guidance counseling.

About the Illustrator

Vicki Diggs is also a West Texas ranch wife. Her husband, Mike, manages the Chimney Creek Ranch near Spur, Texas. She and daughter Erin, 17, and son Zachary, 15, help with ranch work and raise emus, which are similar to ostriches. Ms. Diggs frequently enters her work in art shows and has received numerous awards. Her art has been published in *Western Horseman* and *Texas Hereford Magazine*. She is originally from Roswell, New Mexico, but has lived in Texas for 24 years.

ISBN 1-885777-035

Book design by Janet Long. Manufactured in Hong Kong by South China Printing Co. (1988) Ltd.

McClellan, Doris.
    Baxter Badger's home / written by Doris McClellan ; illustrated by Vicki Diggs.
        p. cm.
    Includes bibliographical references.
    Summary: Every time that Baxter Badger returns from hunting for food at night, he finds his burrow occupied by other animals.
    ISBN 1-885777-03-5 (hc)
    1. Badgers--Juvenile fiction. [1. Badgers--Fiction.] I. Diggs, Vicki, ill. II. Title.
PZ10.3.M1285Bax 1995
[E]--dc20   95-9774
                                      CIP
                                        AC

 Hendrick-Long Publishing Co.

P.O. Box 25123 • Dallas, Texas 75225-1123